# Re
# Cricket

Written by Tom Palmer

Illustrated by Iva Sasheva

 **Collins**

"Out!" Adnan shouted as he caught the ball. Adnan and his friends were playing cricket on the street, using wooden crates as wickets. As Adnan bowled, he dreamt he played for a real cricket club.

3

When it started to rain, Adnan's friends went inside to play Xbox. But Adnan kept on practising, bowling at a wall. He loved cricket too much to let the rain stop him.

When it got too dark, Adnan went inside.
He stared at the posters of cricketers on his
bedroom wall, and wished more than anything
that he could be one himself.

The next day, the sun was shining. Adnan's first ball beat his friend Tahir, smashing the crate. But as Adnan celebrated, he heard a shout. The broken crate had hit a car.

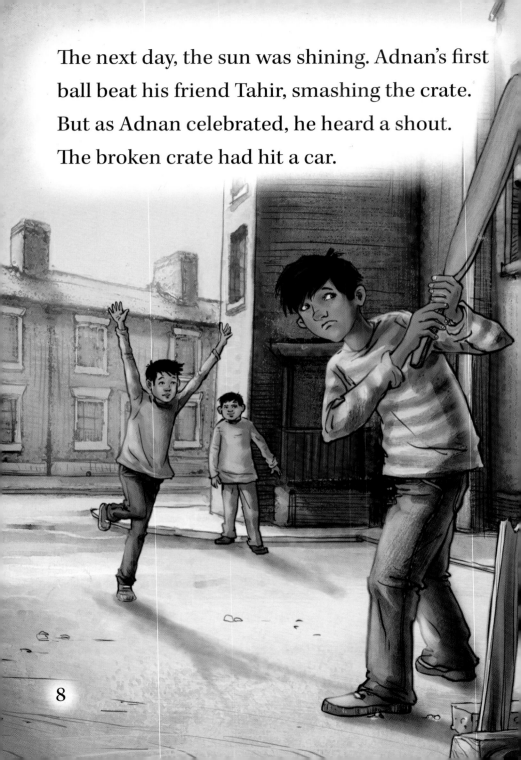

A man wearing cricket whites climbed out.

Adnan realised that the man played
for the local team! But his excitement disappeared
when he saw his stern face.

"Who bowled that ball?" he asked.

"I did," Adnan admitted.

"I need to talk to your parents," the man said.

Adnan's heart sank.

13

Adnan waited in the hall while the man,
Mr Hussain, spoke to his parents. Adnan knew
he'd be in big trouble.

The door finally opened. Adnan's heart skipped a beat.

But his dad, mum and Mr Hussain were all smiling.

"You're an excellent cricketer, Adnan," said
Mr Hussain. "I drive past this street every day
and see you bowling. Would you try out for our
youth team?"

Less than an hour later, Adnan stood on a real cricket pitch with his parents and Mr Hussain watching from the clubhouse.

18

He took a deep breath, ran up and bowled
his first ball.

It hit the wicket! Adnan punched the air. He couldn't believe it! His dream was coming true, and this was just the beginning ...

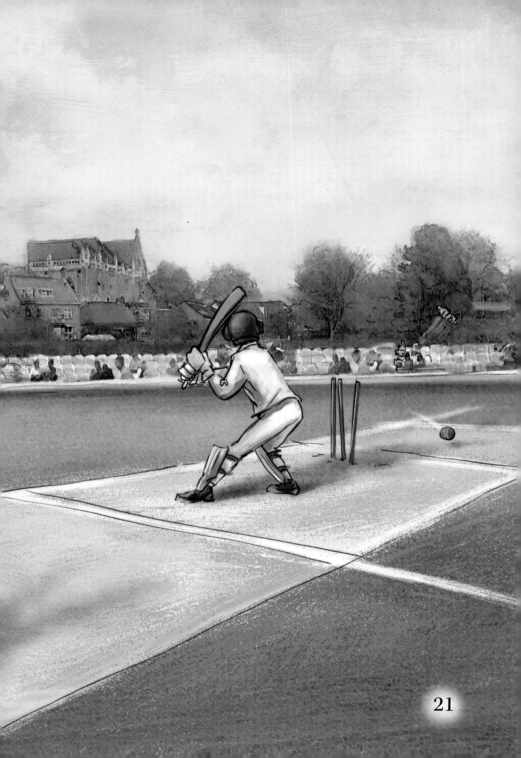

# Making dreams come true

## Saturday

I played cricket with my friends until it rained. After that, I just practised my bowling. I'd love to play for a real cricket team one day, so I have to keep practising.

## Sunday

I bowled Tahir out today with a great ball, but part of the crate we use for a wicket hit a man's car. It was Mr Hussain from the local cricket team!

I thought I was in big trouble when he asked to see my parents. He talked to them for ages. Instead I got a surprise. Mr Hussain asked if I wanted to try out for the youth cricket team! Cool!

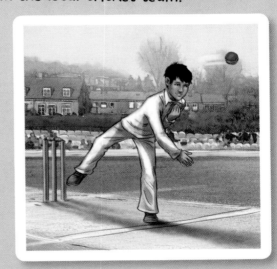

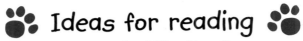

# Ideas for reading

Written by Gillian Howell
*Primary Literacy Consultant*

**Learning objectives:** *(reading objectives correspond with Orange band; all other objectives correspond with Sapphire band)* read independently and with increasing fluency longer and less familiar texts; understand underlying themes, causes and points of view; recognise rhetorical devices used to argue, persuade, mislead and sway the reader; improvise using a range of drama strategies and conventions to explore themes such as hopes, fears and desires

**Curriculum links:** Citizenship, P.E.

**Interest words:** caught, crates, wickets, dreamt, cricketers, celebrated, stern, bowled, excellent, youth

**Resources:** pens, paper, whiteboard

**Word count:** 300

## Getting started

- Check what the children already know about cricket and introduce the sport if needed.

- Read the title together and discuss the illustration on the cover. Ask the children to speculate on what the book will be about, e.g. will it tell a story or give information about cricket? Ask them to give reasons for their opinions.

- Turn to the back cover and read the blurb to confirm the children's ideas. Ask them, based on the blurb, to suggest what might happen in the story. Note their ideas on the whiteboard.

## Reading and responding

- Ask the children to read up to p11 quietly. Listen in as they read and prompt as necessary if they struggle with any words, e.g. celebrated on p8.